To   : _____

From : _____

"Dedicated to the Holy Spirit who led me to write this book, and to mynieces and nephews. May God bless you in all your days."

I Still WILL ALWAYS LOVE YOU

When things are well and you
are happy,
I will always love you.

Even when times are tough and
you are snappy,
I still will always love you.

When skies are clear and the sun shines bright, I will always love you.

Even when thunder roars in the
dark of night,
I still will always love you.

When you try your hardest and
do your best,
I will always love you.

Even when you fail and feel
distressed,
I still will always love you.

When the wind blows soft and
the birds happily sing,
I will always love you.

Even when lightning strikes
with a thunderous ring,
I still will always love you.

When school is out and
it's time to play,
I will always love you.

Even when you throw a fit because you didn't get your way, I still will always love you.

When you sing a song and
make a pretty sound,
I will always love you.

Even when you get really mad
and stomp around,
I still will always love you.

When you eat pumpkin pie and
chocolate cake,
I will always love you.

Even when you fall and make
something break,
I still will always love you.

When you learn to read
and learn to cook,
I will always love you.

Even when you are mad and give me a dirty look, I still will always love you.

When you run outside and
throw the ball,
I will always love you.

Even when you run too fast
and trip and fall,
I still will always love you.

I Still WILL ALWAYS LOVE YOU